Scruff Speaks!

Written by
Elizabeth Dale

Illustrated by
Marta Dorado

Chapter 1

Mia loved going for walks across the moors, especially on wild days like today. Her skin tingled as menacing dark clouds swept across the sky. A storm was coming!

Her dad saw it too.

"Mia!" he called. "We need to head back! Now!"

Mia frowned. What a shame.

It was a long way back to the car. Heavy rain started to fall and, as the wind blew harder, strands of Mia's dark hair whipped across her face.

They were almost there when a lightning flash lit up something white and small racing towards Mia. It was a dog!

"Mia, come on!" called her mum.

But Mia couldn't move. She looked around. There was nobody rushing after the dog, who was all on her own. Mia crouched down, holding out her arms, and the little dog ran towards her, then stopped.

"Hey there," Mia said, soothingly. "You poor thing. Come to me."

Suddenly, there was a resounding crash of thunder overhead and with a yelp the little dog leapt into Mia's arms. Mia held her close and hurried after her parents.

"What have you got there?" her dad asked as Mia climbed into the car.

"A dog! Out on her own," said Mia. The tiny animal cowered in her arms as though trying to hide.

"We can't take a dog home with us!" her dad cried.

"Well, we can't leave her here in this storm!" Mia said. "She's wet through and absolutely terrified."

"Her owner's probably looking for her," said her dad. He jumped out of the car, ran to the fence to look around and then rushed back, absolutely drenched.

"Nobody in sight!" he panted. "And we're the last car here. Is there a name or phone number on her collar?"

Mia peered at the collar. "It's a bit faint. I can just see something like 5...C...R...7...7. Maybe it's Scruff?"

"Of course!" laughed her mum. "Scruff suits her perfectly!"

Scruff whimpered as though she understood.

Mia hugged her. "Poor Scruff!" she said. "Look, Dad, nobody's around to claim her. We can come back early tomorrow and put up a poster to say we found her. Let's go!"

Fortunately he agreed and they set off home, only stopping to buy dog food.

★★★

Scruff was starving! She could hardly wait for Mia to clean off all her mud before wolfing down her dinner. Afterwards, they played together in the lounge. Scruff was very shy, nervously hiding behind the settee when Mia's parents walked in. So Mia took her up to her bedroom to play.

Mia's mum came in at bedtime.

"Isn't Scruff adorable?" Mia said, hugging her.

"Yes," said her mum. "But don't get too attached, darling. I've posted online about her tonight and we'll put up that poster tomorrow. Hopefully her owner will claim her. If not, we'll check if she's chipped."

Mia's face fell. "But if we can't trace her owner... can we keep her?"

Her mum hesitated. "If you show us you can care for her, perhaps it would be nice to have an addition to the family...?"

Mia grinned happily. She would be the best, most caring dog-owner ever!

Chapter 2

Scruff soon fell asleep in the bed Mia made for her, but Mia was too excited. She kept peeping at the little dog, hoping against hope that they wouldn't find the owner—and Scruff could be hers!

Finally, Mia closed her eyes and drifted off to sleep.

"Mia! Help me!"

Mia opened her eyes and looked around. Scruff was staring up at her expectantly.

"Did you hear that, Scruff?" she asked.

"Hear it?! It was *me* speaking!"

Mia was now wide awake. She sat bolt upright, staring at the little dog.

"Did you… did you just speak?" she gasped.

"Yes," said Scruff. "I need your help—urgently!"

"Hold on!" cried Mia. "You're talking… and you're a dog?!"

"Yes. It's very sad."

"Sad?!" exclaimed Mia. "I think it's brilliant!"

"No, it isn't," said Scruff with a shudder. "I've escaped from a horrible, horrible place on the moors where nasty crooks experiment on dogs. They've put a chip in me so I can spy for them and tell them what I see."

Mia moved closer, totally horrified. "No!" she cried.

"There are lots of dogs trapped there. Will you rescue my friend, Rolo, Mia? Please!"

"Of course!" said Mia, jumping up. "I'll ask my parents to help."

"No!" yelled Scruff. "They're big humans like the nasty crooks! All big humans scare me. I can't talk to them."

"Mia?!" called Mia's mum from the landing.

Mia flung herself back into bed, just as her door opened.

"Darling? Are you okay?" asked her mum. "I heard shouting."

"Oh... yes... just a dream," said Mia, stretching. "I'm fine, thanks."

"Good. Sleep well, then."

As soon as her mum left, Mia tried to reassure Scruff. "You can trust both my parents," she whispered.

"No," said Scruff. "They're big humans. You mustn't tell them my secret! Promise me!"

"Okay, I won't," said Mia, hugging her. "I'll help you tomorrow without telling them."

"Thank you."

"Can I ask you about life as a dog?" Mia asked.

"Okay," said Scruff. "Just for five minutes. I'm tired."

So Scruff told her, all about the magical smells there are everywhere and how she can hear sounds from a mile away. How she longed to roam free on the moors.

She explained that she'd escaped when lightning struck the research station, knocking out all power, so the electric fence and locks stopped working. How she'd begged Rolo to come with her but he was too scared.

Scruff whimpered as she recalled her poor friend.

"Don't worry," said Mia. "We'll rescue him tomorrow. I promise. Now go to sleep. You need to rest."

Mia climbed back into bed, her head whirring. She couldn't believe that she had a talking dog... or that somewhere on the moors, other dogs were being experimented on by evil crooks.

Chapter 3

BANG! BANG! BANG!

The loud knocking at the front door woke Mia and Scruff early the next day.

Mia sat up in bed. What was going on?

"We've come about our lovely dog," said a gruff voice. "We rang earlier."

No! Mia stared at Scruff in horror. It was the evil crooks. They must have read her mum's online post.

"We've missed her so much," said another voice.

"I recognise those voices!" Scruff hissed, trembling all over.

"Don't worry, Scruff, I won't let them take you!" said Mia, jumping out of bed.

But she could already hear her dad's footsteps coming up the stairs. She grabbed Scruff and quickly squeezed into the wardrobe with her, just as her dad walked in.

"Oh!" he cried, and went back downstairs. "I'm afraid my daughter must have taken Scruff for a walk," he said.

Not yet I haven't! thought Mia, still clutching Scruff. She grabbed her mobile phone, then tiptoed across the landing, down the stairs and out the back door. The dewy grass was wet and cold on her bare feet, but Mia didn't care.

Mia ran as fast as she could to the back gate and then along the alleyway to her friend Zak's house.

She threw a pebble up at his bedroom window and soon his sleepy face appeared.

"Mia!" he laughed, opening the window. "What are you doing?! You're barefoot! In your pink unicorn pyjamas! With a dog!"

"Shh!" Mia hissed. "No one must know I'm here. You have to help me, Zak. It's urgent!"

"How?" he asked.

"We're going on a rescue mission to save trapped dogs. Can you get me a jacket and trainers, please? And can I borrow your sister's bike?"

"Er... okay... I guess."

"But don't tell her," said Mia. "Or your mum. I'll see you behind the garage. Please hurry!"

Fortunately, Jenny's bike had a basket. Mia popped Scruff in it and wheeled it out of the garage, just as Zak joined her and handed her the jacket and shoes.

"Where are we going?" he asked, fetching his bike.

"Up on the moors," said Mia, putting on the trainers.

"Okay! Hang on..." said Zak, nipping back into his house.

Mia frowned. What was he doing?!

Zak reappeared with a huge rucksack.

"Provisions!" he grinned as Mia started cycling.

"So, tell me what's going on?" he yelled, leaping on

his bike and overtaking her as she wobbled along on

Jenny's little bike.

"Hold on!" she panted. "It's hard trying to stay on this thing. I keep bashing my knees on the handlebars."

Mia had to pedal the little wheels twice as fast as Zak to keep up with him. All the time she was terrified that one of the passing cars might contain the nasty crooks looking for Scruff. Finally they reached the moors' car park and she was glad to jump off the bike.

"Time for snacks now?" asked Zak.

"No," said Mia. "Let's get onto the moors! Come on, Scruff!" And she lifted the little dog out of the basket.

Chapter 4

Luckily, it was too early for many people to be about. When they'd gone far enough, Mia sat down and let Scruff run around. The little dog quickly found a stream and drank thirstily from it.

"Crisps or chocolate?" Zak asked Mia, holding out both.

"I see you're eating healthily as usual!" she laughed, taking both. She was starving.

"I brought some sausages for your dog if he'd like them?" Zak asked.

"Yes please!" called Scruff, running back—fast!

Zak nearly fell over. "Your dog—he just talked!"

"Yes!" Mia laughed.

"But... but... he can't!"

"Yes I can!" said Scruff. "And please stop calling me 'he'. I'm a 'she' and proud of it! Where are those sausages?"

Zak couldn't move, so Scruff sniffed them out for herself. Zak stared at her, stunned. "How... how...?"

So Mia told him the full story.

"How awful!" Zak said. "So, tell me what it's like being a dog, Scruff. Is it fun?"

"Not at the research station," Scruff answered. "Come on, we've got to rescue Rolo!"

"Okay," said Zak, stuffing chocolate in his mouth and biscuits in his pocket. "Where is the research station?"

"Over there... somewhere," said Scruff, looking round vaguely. "I'm sure I can find it."

But she didn't sound quite sure. Mia frowned at Zak, but Scruff scurried off, so they followed her wagging tail as she made her way through the heather. At first, she was very enthusiastic and they had to run to keep up with her. But after a while she paused at a big grassy patch.

"Are you going the right way, Scruff?" Mia asked her. "When I met you, you weren't coming from over here."

"Oh," said Scruff. "You may be right. Everywhere smelt different when it was wet."

Mia sank onto the grass. They were getting nowhere fast and her toes were sore where Zak's old trainers were rubbing them. Zak flopped down beside her as she gingerly examined her blisters. Then she looked up.

"Where's Scruff?" she asked.

Zak stood up and pointed. "There!" he cried. "Scruff! Come back!"

But Scruff disappeared round the side of the hill.

"No!" Mia wailed. "Go after her, Zak!"

Zak set off, while Mia quickly put her trainers back on and ran after him. But they couldn't see Scruff anywhere.

"It's useless," Zak called. "She's so tiny, she gets lost among all the heather. And she can't see far from down there. She'll never find the research station."

"And we might never find her!" said Mia. "Oh, Scruff! I'm sorry, I've let you down..."

Chapter 5

Mia closed her eyes in despair, and then she heard a loud bark. Scruff was racing back round the hillside! Thank goodness!

"I've found it!" Scruff cried. "I've found the research station."

"Clever girl!" Mia laughed.

Her blisters didn't hurt anymore as she and Zak ran after the little dog. Suddenly, they could see a tall chimney. It was still a long way away, but at least they knew where they were heading!

The big, dark grey building looked really ominous as they approached it. There was a high wall surrounding it, with a tall gate and a car parked outside. They could hear loud barking.

"They're exercising!" said Scruff, excitedly racing ahead.

"Scruff! Come back!" Mia cried. "The crooks mustn't see you. They'll catch you again! Hide under this bush. Leave the rescue to us!"

"No!" said Scruff. "I have to show you which dog is Rolo."

"Then hide in my rucksack," said Zak. "I've eaten all the snacks so there's room. Mia, stand by the wall where the barbed wire is missing. I'll climb on your shoulders then, with Scruff in my rucksack, we should both be able to see over it."

Mia hesitated, but what else could they do? "Be careful!" she said.

She crouched down by the wall. Zak carefully stood on her shoulders and Mia gingerly straightened up whilst Zak clung to the wall for support. Finally he—and Scruff—could see over the top.

"There!" Scruff whispered to Zak. "Rolo's the sausage dog in the corner! There are no crooks. You can get him!"

"Right," said Zak, carefully lowering the rucksack to Mia.

"But how are you going to get in?" asked Mia. "Zak! You can't..."

But even as she spoke, Zak pulled himself up onto the top of the wall and jumped down the other side. Horrified, Mia ran and peered through a crack in the gate. She could just see Zak, crouched down, whispering to a sausage dog, who then followed Zak to the gate. Mia stepped back as Zak unbolted it.

As soon as they appeared, Scruff jumped out of Zak's rucksack and bounded up to her friend.

"Rolo! Rolo!" she whispered excitedly. "You're free!"

Chapter 6

"Well done!" Mia told Zak.

But he frowned. "Those other poor dogs!" he said.

"We can't leave them there. We have to set them all

free."

"No!" said Mia, pulling out her mobile. "If we're lucky, we'll escape with Rolo. If you go back in, the crooks might see you and catch Rolo and Scruff." She started dialling. "I'm ringing the police."

But suddenly, they both heard an agonised whine. A poor dog was obviously in pain.

"I have to help them!" Zak cried. "There's nobody about. Now's my chance!"

And before she could stop him, Zak dashed back through the gate.

Almost immediately, Mia heard a shout and a cry from Zak. The crooks must have seen him!

"Hide! Quick!" Mia hissed to Rolo and Scruff before rushing through the gate to help Zak. But someone grabbed her arm from behind straight away, knocking her mobile from her hand. As Mia desperately struggled to wriggle free, the man's grip tightened and then she saw the most terrible sight: Scruff running past her—straight into a metal cage. No! Silly dog! She just hoped that Rolo didn't follow her!

As she and Zak were tied to the same pole, Mia felt terrible. This was her fault! She'd dialled the numbers, if she'd actually put through her call to the police, they could have been on their way now and they'd all be rescued.

"You have been very silly children!" a man snarled.

"Now we'll have to decide what to do with you."

Mia watched miserably as he and his colleague shut

all the other dogs in their cages that surrounded the

yard. They all looked so sad. Poor Scruff was hiding

in a far corner of her cage, with her back to Mia.

When the crooks went into the building, Zak and Mia could talk freely. They both blamed themselves for messing up the rescue and wondered what would happen to them.

"Maybe they won't realise Scruff's talked to us or that we know what they're up to?" said Zak, hopefully. "Maybe they'll set us free?"

"Maybe," said Mia. But, in her heart, she didn't believe it. And as hours went by, as they stood there, growing cold and hungry, any hope of a quick release disappeared. Were the crooks waiting until it was dark to move them? Where to? Mia knew her parents would be desperately worried. She looked around for her mobile, but it was nowhere to be seen. The crooks must have picked it up. Even if her parents rang her, the horrible thugs wouldn't answer.

Chapter 7

Dusk descended, and Mia had lost all hope of being set free when suddenly she heard loud sirens. She and Zak looked at each other, eyes wide. It was the police! It had to be! They watched, horrified, as the crooks dashed out of their building and through the gate towards their car. No! They were escaping!

Five minutes later, police came through the gate— leading the thugs in handcuffs!

"Over here!" Zak yelled.

"You caught the nasty crooks!" Mia cried.

"Brilliant! We thought they'd escaped."

"They would have done," said a policewoman. "But their tyres were torn to shreds."

Mia frowned. How odd. And then Rolo came running over, tail wagging, with a bit of black rubber in his mouth.

"Rolo!" Zak cried. "You clever dog!"

"We had no idea this place was here," said a policeman, as he untied them. "Thank you for ringing us, but you really should have waited for us to arrive rather than rushing in and taking matters into your own hands."

Mia and Zak looked at each other, puzzled.

"But we didn't ring you," said Mia.

"Are you Mia?" the policeman asked.

"Yes..."

"Well, someone named Mia rang," he said.

This was getting stranger than ever!

"Whoever it was who called, told us all about this terrible place and that you were being kept hostage. Mind you, if the directions hadn't been so awful, we'd have got here much sooner!"

Mia couldn't believe what she was hearing. And then she saw Scruff, scurrying out of her cage, holding a mobile in her mouth. And everything became clear.

She ran over to her and Zak followed. "It was you, Scruff, wasn't it?!" Mia said.

Scruff dropped Mia's mobile at her feet. "Yes," she whispered. "Through the open gate, I saw you drop your phone, so I dashed in and picked it up. You'd said you were ringing the police, so I carried it into the cage where the crooks would leave me alone and wouldn't hear me talking to them. When I saw that you hadn't pressed dial, I pressed it with my nose. And when a big human answered, I couldn't say I was a dog, could I? So I pretended to be you."

"Brilliant, Scruff!" Zak cried.

"Yes!" said Mia. "How clever of you to make the call. And I can't believe you actually overcame your fear and spoke to adults! Brave little Scruff!"

Scruff wagged her tail. "Once was enough though," she said. "Don't ask me to do it again!"

"I won't!" Mia laughed. "I'm so proud of you, Scruff. Thanks to you, all these dogs will be rescued and find lovely new homes. And I'll do my utmost to make sure that you and Rolo come and live with me—so from now on, you can save all your talking for me!"

"And me!" Zak added.

"Of course!" Scruff said happily and Mia gave her a big hug.

They were going to share the best secret ever!

Discussion Points

1. Where did Mia find Scruff at the beginning of the story?

2. Why was Scruff running away?

a) She was scared of the lightning

b) She was escaping evil crooks

c) She was being naughty

I am Dogicorn!

3. What was your favourite part of the story?

4. How did Mia, Scruff and Zac save Rolo?

5. Why do you think Mia thought that Scruff's ability to talk was great?

6. Who was your favourite character and why?

7. There were moments in the story when Mia was **helpful**. Where do you think the story shows this most?

8. What do you think happens after the end of the story?

Book Bands for Guided Reading

The Institute of Education book banding system is a scale of colours that reflects the various levels of reading difficulty. The bands are assigned by taking into account the content, the language style, the layout and phonics. Word, phrase and sentence level work is also taken into consideration.

The Maverick Readers Scheme is a bright, attractive range of books covering the pink to grey bands. All of these books have been book banded for guided reading to the industry standard and edited by a leading educational consultant.

To view the whole Maverick Readers scheme, visit our website at

www.maverickearlyreaders.com

Or scan the QR code to view our scheme instantly!

Maverick Chapter Readers

(From Lime to Grey Band)